18 GREATEST
SCIENCE FICTION STORIES

Here are stories of imagination, stories which transport the reader beyond space and into strange worlds of wonder—picked by the major writers, editors, experts in this field. Among others, you will read about . . .

an exploring party on a frontier planet . . .

a boy whose power to kill by thought changes the world . . .

an android who faces an ancient magic . . .

a matter converter which changes the Earth beyond recognition . . .

an automated house which makes parents unnecessary . . .

a mind-reading robot . . .

the custodian of the world's treasures and his last days on Earth before the Sun goes nova . . .

This Tempo Books *edition contains the complete text of the original hard-cover edition.*

18 Greatest Science Fiction Stories

(Originally titled: Masters' Choice)

Edited by LAURENCE M. JANIFER

TEMPO
BOOKS

GROSSET & DUNLAP
A NATIONAL GENERAL COMPANY
New York

CONTENTS

The author and publisher gratefully acknowledge permission from the following to reprint:

LIAR!, by Isaac Asimov, copyright 1941 by Street & Smith Publications, Inc. First appeared in *Astounding Science Fiction*, May 1941. Reprinted by permission of the author.

IT'S A *Good* LIFE, by Jerome Bixby, copyright 1953 by Ballantine Books, Inc. Reprinted by permission of the author.

THE VELDT, by Ray Bradbury, copyright 1950 by the Curtis Publishing Company, Inc. Reprinted by permission of the Harold Matson Co., Inc.

THE GOLEM, by Avram Davidson, copyright 1955 by Fantasy House, Inc.; reprinted by permission of the author and the author's agents, Scott Meredith Literary Agency, Inc.

HELEN O'LOY, by Lester del Rey, copyright 1938 by Street & Smith Publications, Inc.; reprinted by permission of the author and the author's agents, Scott Meredith Literary Agency, Inc.

THE COLD EQUATIONS, by Tom Godwin, copyright 1954 by Street & Smith Publications, Inc. Reprinted by permission of the author's agent, Theron Raines.

THE DWINDLING SPHERE, by Willard Hawkins, copyright 1940 by Street & Smith Publications, Inc. Reprinted by permission of the author.

REQUIEM, by Robert A. Heinlein, copyright 1939 by Street & Smith Publications, Inc., originally published in *Astounding Science Fiction*. Reprinted by permission of the author.

THEORY OF ROCKETRY, by C. M. Kornbluth, copyright 1958 by Fantasy House, Inc. Reprinted by permission of the Estate of C. M. Kornbluth.

DON'T LOOK NOW, by Henry Kuttner, copyright 1948 by Better Publications, Inc. Reprinted by permission of the Harold Matson Co., Inc.

SEVEN-DAY TERROR, by R. A. Lafferty, copyright 1962 by Galaxy Publishing Corp. Reprinted by permission of the author.

COMING ATTRACTION, by Fritz Leiber, copyright 1950 by World Editions, Inc. Reprinted by permission of the author.

POLITICS, by Murray Leinster, copyright *Astounding Stories*, 1932. Reprinted by permission of the author.

MEMENTO HOMO, by Walter M. Miller, Jr., copyright 1954 by Ziff Davis Publishing Co. Reprinted by permission of the Harold Matson Co., Inc.

THE BRIGHT ILLUSION, by C. L. Moore, copyright 1934 by Street & Smith Publications, Inc. Reprinted by permission of the Harold Matson Co., Inc.

AND NOW THE NEWS, by Theodore Sturgeon, copyright 1956 by Fantasy House, Inc. Reprinted by permission of the author.

THE CUSTODIAN, by William Tenn, copyright 1953 by Quinn Publishing Company, Inc. Originally appeared in *If*. Reprinted by permission of Philip Klass.

PREFACE

The basic form of science fiction, for a great many years, was the short story. There are a variety of reasons for this. One of them, at least, is that only in magazines, which could be satisfied with a smaller percentage of sales, was science fiction at all acceptable. Very few book publishers in the 1930s and 1940s were experimenting with this sort of stuff, and those few were mostly small houses which could not pay the writer enough to keep him even slightly solvent. The writer of science fiction, typically, was then a man who wrote for the magazines. The days of André Norton, Edgar Pangborn and others whose main reputations came from the hard-cover or the paperback novel were yet to come, and the days of the great originals—Wells, Verne, Stapledon—were gone. During what is now called the Golden Age of science fiction, the magazine reigned supreme, and the short story was its backbone.

The natural result of this parade of extremely perishable pulp paper has been the appearance of the anthology. I have no idea how many anthologies have been published in this country alone within our field. Walter Cole's *Checklist of Science-Fiction Anthologies* is an enormous volume filled with nothing but the contents pages of various such works, each displaying what the individual editor thinks science fiction is, or thinks it ought to be—or, in the simplest possible terms of the problem, what the editor thinks he can sell as science fiction to a reasonably numerous reading public.

This anthology (not as an excuse, but in the way of explanation) is a little different. The stories contained herein, and the Honor Roll at the back of the book, do not concern themselves with what I think science fiction is; they concern themselves with what science fiction thinks science fiction is. Twenty-three major authors and editors in the field were asked to provide a list of five stores which they felt worthy of inclusion in this Honor Roll as among the best of all time. (Three of these refused, on the perfectly reasonable ground that it required altogether too much work.) To the twenty whose lists I've got I can only try to convey my amazement at their willingness to do the work, and my heartfelt gratitude.

The voting lists ranged in length from two stories to thirty-two, and, although there was some attempt on my part to keep the stories nominated as short as possible, individual pieces as long as 35,000 words were listed. This made for problems, and I've been forced to leave out a great number of very popular stories, which is more regrettable than I can say. Unfortunately, there is a limit to the amount of words that can be packed into one volume.

This anthology, then, consists of stories which were selected from the Honor Roll on various bases: the number of votes received for each story, the comparative availability of a story (where possible, I've tried to pick less familiar works), and the total number of votes for a given author. Personal choice (which is to say mine) played a small but definitive part for which I offer no excuse whatever.

To print the entire Honor Roll would have required a small five-foot shelf. To print only those stories which were currently unavailable, or, again, only those which received the most votes, would have been a disservice to any picture of the field as a whole—which picture I hope this anthology can begin to provide. Where several of an author's stories were nominated, but no single story seemed to bulk especially large in the nominators' minds to the exclusion of others, I've made, simply, what choice I could, and tried to explain that choice in the introduction to the story.

It ought to go without saying that any opinions expressed here, or in the introductions to the various stories, are mine; the authors whose stories were chosen, or the authors and editors who did the choosing, are not responsible; the publishers are not responsible; the printers (except by inadvertence) are not responsible; and I don't feel so well myself.

However . . .

The question, after all these years, remains: what is science fiction? Every writer and every editor in the field seems to have his own definition, and most of them appear to cherish a desire to get rid of the term entirely. I don't have any particular animus against the words "science fiction," either separately or together, and I think we might as well stick to the phrase as a label—since, eventually, it will mean what you put into it, and nothing else.

But what have we put into it? Well, more and more, science fiction seems to me to separate itself into three distinct forms, and three distinct kinds of literature. The first sort, of which "The Dwindling Sphere," "Politics" and "Don't Look Now" can serve as handy examples, is what the fan or regular reader usually means when he uses the term. These are stories dealing with ourselves and with the societies we variously live in, looking, in that set of frameworks, at a new invention, a new concept, a strange society or a strange being. The viewpoint, however odd the material, remains the normal viewpoint of the author's society at the time of writing: he may approve or disapprove the novelty at which he's looking —he may, for that matter, approve or disapprove the society through which he's looking at it—but he takes his stand for reasons normally available and in currency within the society by which he's surrounded. Quite a lot of this type is being written, most of it for science-fiction magazines and a very little of it for the major mass-circulation-magazine markets. Most new science-fiction novels are of this type. It does not, however, seem to be increasing in quantity; it remains the standard form, and has become a form whose sales are small, steady and predictable, like the standard detective story.

The second type is here, too, in such different stories as "The Golem," "And Now the News" and "The Veldt." These stories take as their model something which was not originally a part of the field: the quality story, the little-magazine story, and the story or novel for which critical acclaim is seen as a more urgent factor than high sales. This type of story is not on the increase, either: it can't increase. Such stories rapidly become indistinguishable from the field in which they reside, the little-magazine field, and glad cries go up from here and there to the effect that science fiction is being accepted. It isn't: it's being diluted in the mainstream, as our critics are fond of calling it—as, in quite a different way, the picaresque novel was lost in the novel proper.

The third type, though, is quite independent. Such stories as "Coming Attraction," "Theory of Rocketry" and, in its own strange way, "The Bright Illusion" take their initial stand in an alien environment and judge both their own environment and ours by standards which may not meet either present or popular approval—standards which may not be visible at all within any actual society. In such stories as these (and a few novels of the same sort), the—overly familiar—"sense of wonder" is given free play and, since it is the living basis of all fiction, illuminates the work. The reader is given the opportunity of truly new experience, in an alien mode, and, therefore, the chance to widen his own background and his own equipment for judgment and for appreciation. It seems to me that there are more stories and novels of this sort around now than there used to be, and that, if science fiction is experiencing a real growth in any direction, this is it. It appears to require a stronger mind, and a less limited one, than most writers in the field have to succeed with a story of this type—just as the growth of a certain amount of literacy in the field forced its own higher standards.

So much for argument.

Even more than the usual literary work, an anthology is, in however unrecognized a manner, a collaborative effort. Without a great many different jobs done by a great many different people, this book would not have been possible. I want to thank a few of them here, with deep appreciation: Miss Barbara Norville and Mr. Clayton Rawson of Simon and Schuster, both very present helps in time of trouble; Mr. Philip Klass, the Gadfly of the Western World, for encouragement, argument and faith; Mr. Walter Cole, whose *Checklist* was a constant aid, and whose assistance far overstepped its bounds; Mr. Jim Sanders, science-fiction fan and collector of index cards; and, most particularly, Miss Greer Aladàr Russell, without whom neither the anthology nor the anthologist might have survived.

Laurence M. Janifer

Liar!

ISAAC ASIMOV

I sometimes have the feeling that a twenty-first-century school child, when asked who invented the robot which will be a common feature of his daily life, is going to answer, "Dr. Isaac Asimov of the Boston University School of Medicine." Actually, Dr. Asimov didn't even invent the robot in science fiction; the credit apparently ought to go to Eando Binder, or possibly to Karel Capek. But Dr. Asimov, creator of the Three Laws of Robotics, has certainly done more about the idea of the robot than anyone else in the field.

"Liar!" is an unusual story even for Dr. Asimov. It is difficult to imagine a crossbreeding between his robots and the tragic heroes of Graham Greene, but here it is: a retelling of "The Heart of the Matter," if slightly revised.

Alfred Lanning lit his cigar carefully, but the tips of his fingers were trembling slightly. His gray eyebrows hunched low as he spoke between puffs.

"It reads minds all right—damn little doubt about that! But why?" He looked at mathematician Peter Bogert. "Well?"

Bogert flattened his black hair down with both hands. "That was the thirty-fourth RB model we've turned out, Lanning. All the others were strictly orthodox."

The third man at the table frowned. Milton Ashe was the youngest officer of U. S. Robot and Mechanical Men, Inc., and proud of his post.

"Listen, Bogert. There wasn't a hitch in the assembly from start to finish. I guarantee that."

Bogert's thick lips spread in a patronizing smile. "Do you? If you can answer for the entire assembly line, I recommend your promotion. By exact count, there are seventy-five thousand, two hundred and thirty-four operations necessary for the manufacture of a single positronic brain, each separate operating depending for successful completion upon any number of factors, from five to a hundred and five. If any one of them goes seriously wrong, the 'brain' is ruined. I quote our own information folder, Ashe."

Milton Ashe flushed, but a fourth voice cut off his reply.

"If we're going to start by trying to fix the blame on one another, I'm leaving." Susan Calvin's hands were folded tightly in her lap, and the little lines about her thin, pale lips deepened. "We've got a mind-reading robot on our hands and it strikes me as rather important that we find out just why it reads minds. We're not going to do that by saying, 'Your fault! My fault!' "

Her cold gray eyes fastened upon Ashe and he grinned.

Lanning grinned too, and, as always at such times, his long white hair and shrewd little eyes made him the picture of a Biblical patriarch. "True for you, Dr. Calvin." His voice became suddenly crisp. "Here's everything in pill-concentrate form. We've produced a positronic brain of supposedly ordinary vintage that's got a remarkable property of being able to tune in on thought waves. It would mark the most important advance in robotics in decades if we knew how it happened. We don't, and we have to find out. Is that clear?"

"May I make a suggestion?" asked Bogert.

"Go ahead!"

"I'd say that until we do figure out the mess—and as a mathematician I expect it to be a very devil of a mess—we keep the existence of RB-34 a secret. I mean even from the other members of the staff. As heads of the departments, we ought not to find it an insoluble problem, and the fewer know about it . . ."

"Bogert is right," said Dr. Calvin. "Ever since the Interplanetary Code was modified to allow robot models to be tested in the plants before being shipped out to space, antirobot propaganda has increased. If any word leaks out about a robot being able to read minds before we can announce complete control of the phenomenon, pretty effective capital would be made out of it."

Lanning sucked at his cigar and nodded gravely. He turned to Ashe. "I think you said you were alone when you first stumbled on this thought-reading business."

"I'll say I was alone—I got the scare of my life. RB-34 had just been taken off the assembly table and they sent him down to me. Obermann was off somewheres, so I took him down to the testing rooms myself—at least I started to take him down." Ashe paused, and a tiny smile tugged at his lips. "Say, did any of you ever carry on a thought conversation without knowing it?"

No one bothered to answer, and he continued. "You don't realize it at first, you know. He just spoke to me—as logically and sensibly as you can imagine—and it was only when I was most of the way down to the testing rooms that I realized that I hadn't said anything. Sure, I thought lots, but that isn't the same thing, is it? I locked that thing up and ran for Lanning. Having it walking beside me, calmly peering into my thoughts and picking and choosing among them, gave me the willies."

"I imagine it would," said Susan Calvin thoughtfully. Her eyes fixed themselves upon Ashe in an oddly intent manner. "We are so accustomed to considering our own thoughts private."

Lanning broke in impatiently. "Then only the four of us know. All right! We've got to go about this systematically. Ashe, I want you to check over the assembly line from beginning to end—everything. You're to eliminate all operations in which there was no possible chance of an error, and list all those where there were, together with its nature and possible magnitude."

"Tall order," grunted Ashe.

"Naturally! Of course you're to put the men under you to work on this—every single one if you have to, and I don't care if we go behind schedule, either. But they're not to know why, you understand."

"Hm-m-m, yes!" The young technician grinned wryly. "It's still a lulu of a job."

Lanning swiveled about in his chair and faced Calvin. "You'll have to tackle the job from the other direction. You're the robopsychologist of the plant, so you're to study the robot itself and work backward. Try to find out how he ticks. See what else is tied up with his telepathic powers, how far they extend, how they warp his outlook, and just exactly what harm it has done to his ordinary RB properties. You've got that?"

3

Lanning didn't wait for Dr. Calvin to answer. "I'll co-ordinate the work and interpret the findings mathematically." He puffed violently at his cigar and mumbled the rest through the smoke. "Bogert will help me there, of course."

Bogert polished the nails of one pudgy hand with the other and said blandly, "I daresay. I know a little in the line."

"Well! I'll get started." Ashe shoved his chair back and rose. His pleasantly youthful face crinkled in a grin. "I've got the darnedest job of any of us, so I'm getting out of here and to work." He left with a slurred "B' seein' ye!"

Susan Calvin answered with a barely perceptible nod, but her eyes followed him out of sight and she did not answer when Lanning grunted and said, "Do you want to go up and see RB-34 now, Dr. Calvin?"

RB-34's photoelectric eyes lifted from the book at the muffled sound of hinges turning, and he was upon his feet when Susan Calvin entered.

She paused to readjust the huge "No Entrance" sign upon the door and then approached the robot.

"I've brought you the texts upon hyperatomic motors, Herbie—a few, anyway. Would you care to look at them?"

RB-34—otherwise known as Herbie—lifted the three heavy books from her arms and opened to the title page of one.

"Hm-m-m! 'Theory of Hyperatomics.' " He mumbled inarticulately to himself as he flipped the pages, and then spoke with an abstracted air. "Sit down, Dr. Calvin! This will take me a few minutes."

The psychologist seated herself and watched Herbie narrowly as he took a chair at the other side of the table and went through the three books systematically.

At the end of half an hour he put them down. "Of course, I know why you brought these."

The corner of Dr. Calvin's lip twitched. "I was afraid you would. It's difficult to work with you, Herbie. You're always a step ahead of me."

"It's the same with these books, you know, as with the others. They just don't interest me. There's nothing to your textbooks. Your science is just a mass of collected data plastered together by makeshift theory—and all so incredibly simple that it's scarcely worth bothering about. It's your fiction that interests me. Your studies of the interplay of human motives and emotions . . ." His mighty hand gestured vaguely as he sought the proper words.

Dr. Calvin whispered, "I think I understand."

"I see into minds, you see," the robot continued, "and you have no idea how complicated they are. I can't begin to understand everything, because my own mind has so little in common with them—but I try, and your novels help."

"Yes, but I'm afraid that after going through some of the harrowing emotional experiences of our present-day sentimental novel"—there was a tinge of bitterness in her voice— "you find real minds like ours dull and colorless."

"But I don't!"

The sudden energy in the response brought the other to her feet. She felt herself reddening, and thought wildly, He must know!

Herbie subsided suddenly and muttered in a low voice from which the metallic timbre departed almost entirely, "But of course I know about it, Dr. Calvin. You think of it always, so how can I help but know?"

Her face was hard. "Have you—told anyone?"

"Of course not!" This with genuine surprise. "No one has asked me."

"Well, then," she flung out, "I suppose you think I am a fool."

"No! It is a normal emotion."

"Perhaps that is why it is so foolish." The wistfulness in her voice drowned out everything else. Some of the woman peered through the layer of doctorhood. "I am not what you would call—attractive."

"If you are referring to mere physical attraction, I couldn't judge. But I know, in any case, that there are other types of attraction."

"Nor young." Dr. Calvin had scarcely heard the robot.

"You are not yet forty." An anxious insistence had crept into Herbie's voice.

"Thirty-eight as you count the years; a shriveled sixty as far as my emotional outlook on life is concerned. Am I a psychologist for nothing?" She drove on with bitter breathlessness. "And he's barely thirty-five and looks and acts younger. Do you suppose he ever sees me as anything but . . . but what I am?"

"You are wrong!" Herbie's steel fist struck the plastic-topped table with a strident clang. "Listen to me—"

But Susan Calvin whirled on him now, and the hunted pain in her eyes became a blaze. "Why should I? What do you know about it all, anyway, you . . . you machine. I'm just a specimen to you; an interesting bug with a peculiar mind spread-eagled for inspection. It's a wonderful example of frustration, isn't it? Almost as good as your books." Her voice, emerging in dry sobs, choked into silence.

The robot cowered at the outburst. He shook his head pleadingly. "Won't you listen to me, please? I could help you if you would let me."

"How?" Her lips curled. "By giving me good advice?"

"No, not that. It's just that I know what other people think —Milton Ashe, for instance."

There was a long silence, and Susan Calvin's eyes dropped. "I don't want to know what he thinks," she gasped. "Keep quiet."

"I think you would want to know what he thinks."

Her head remained bent, but her breath came more quickly. "You are talking nonsense," she whispered.

"Why should I? I am trying to help. Milton Ashe's thought of you—" he paused.

And then the psychologist raised her head. "Well?"

The robot said quietly, "He loves you."

For a full minute Dr. Calvin did not speak. She merely stared. Then: "You are mistaken! You must be. Why should he?"

"But he does. A thing like that cannot be hidden, not from me."

"But I am so . . . so—" she stammered to a halt.

"He looks deeper than the skin, and admires intellect in others. Milton Ashe is not the type to marry a head of hair and a pair of eyes."

Susan Calvin found herself blinking rapidly and waited before speaking. Even then her voice trembled. "Yet he certainly never in any way indicated—"

"Have you ever given him a chance?"

"How could I? I never thought that—"

"Exactly!"

The psychologist paused in thought and then looked up suddenly. "A girl visited him here at the plant half a year ago.

She was pretty, I suppose—blond and slim. And, of course, could scarcely add two and two. He spent all day puffing out his chest, trying to explain how a robot was put toegther." The hardness had returned. "Not that she understood! Who was she?"

Herbie answered without hesitation, "I know the person you are referring to. She is his first cousin, and there is no romantic interest there, I assure you."

Susan Calvin rose to her feet with a vivacity almost girlish. "Now, isn't that strange? That's exactly what I used to pretend to myself sometimes, though I never really thought so. Then it all must be true."

She ran to Herbie and seized his cold, heavy hand in both hers. "Thank you, Herbie." Her voice was an urgent, husky whisper. "Don't tell anyone about this. Let it be our secret—and thank you again." With that, and a convulsive squeeze of Herbie's unresponsive metal fingers, she left.

Herbie turned slowly to his neglected novel, but there was no one to read *his* thoughts.

Milton Ashe stretched slowly and magnificently, to the tune of cracking joints and a chorus of grunts, and then glared at Peter Bogert, Ph.D.

"Say," he said, "I've been at this for a week now with just about no sleep. How long do I have to keep it up? I thought you said the positronic bombardment in Vac Chamber D was the solution."

Bogert yawned delicately and regarded his white hands with interest. "It is. I'm on the track."

"I know what *that* means when a mathematician says it. How near the end are you?"

"It all depends."

"On what?" Ashe dropped into a chair and stretched his long legs out before him.

"On Lanning. The old fellow disagrees with me." He sighed. "A bit behind the times, that's the trouble with him. He clings to matrix mechanics as the all in all, and this problem calls for more powerful mathematical tools. He's so stubborn."

Ashe muttered sleepily, "Why not ask Herbie and settle the whole affair?"

"Ask the robot?" Bogert's eyebrows climbed.

"Why not? Didn't the old girl tell you?"

"You mean Calvin?"

"Yeah! Susie herself. That robot's a mathematical wiz. He knows all about everything plus a bit on the side. He does triple integrals in his head and eats up tensor analysis for dessert."

The mathematician stared skeptically, "Are you serious?"

"So help me! The catch is that the dope doesn't like math. He would rather read slushy novels. Honest! You should see the tripe Susie keeps feeding him: *Purple Passion* and *Love in Space.*"

"Dr. Calvin hasn't said a word of this to us."

"Well, she hasn't finished studying him. You know how she is. She likes to have everything just so before letting out the big secret."

"She's told *you.*"

"We sort of got to talking. I have been seeing a lot of her lately." He opened his eyes wide and frowned. "Say, Bogie, have you been noticing anything queer about the lady lately?"

Bogert relaxed into an undignified grin. "She's using lipstick, if that's what you mean."

"Hell, I know that. Rouge, powder and eye shadow too. She's a sight. But it's not that. I can't put my finger on it. It's the way she talks—as if she were happy about something." He thought a little and then shrugged.

The other allowed himself a leer, which, for a scientist past fifty, was not a bad job. "Maybe she's in love."

Ashe allowed his eyes to close again. "You're nuts, Bogie. You go speak to Herbie; I want to stay here and go to sleep."

"Right! Not that I particularly like having a robot tell me my job, nor that I think he can do it!"

A soft snore was his only answer.

Herbie listened carefully as Peter Bogert, hands in pockets, spoke with elaborate indifference.

"So there you are. I've been told you understand these things, and I am asking you more in curiosity than anything else. My line of reasoning, as I have outlined it, involves a few doubtful steps, I admit, which Dr. Lanning refuses to accept, and the picture is still rather incomplete."

The robot didn't answer, and Bogert said, "Well?"

"I see no mistake," Herbie studied the scribbled figures.

"I don't suppose you can go any further than that?"

"I daren't try. You are a better mathematician than I, and —well, I'd hate to commit myself."

There was a shade of complacency in Bogert's smile. "I rather thought that would be the case. It is deep. We'll forget it." He crumpled the sheets, tossed them down the waste shaft, turned to leave, and then thought better of it. "By the way . . ."

The robot waited.

Bogert seemed to have difficulty. "There is something—that is, perhaps you can—" He stopped.

Herbie spoke quietly. "Your thoughts are confused, but there is no doubt at all that they concern Dr. Lanning. It is silly to hesitate, for as soon as you compose yourself I'll know what it is you want to ask."

The mathematician's hand went to his sleek hair in the familiar smoothing gesture. "Lanning is nudging seventy," he said, as if that explained everything.

"I know that."

"And he's been director of the plant for almost thirty years." Herbie nodded.

"Well, now—" Bogert's voice became ingratiating—"you would know whether . . . whether he's thinking of resigning. Health, perhaps, or some other—"

"Quite," said Herbie, and that was all.

"Well, do you know?"

"Certainly."

"Then—uh—could you tell me?"

"Since you ask, yes." The robot was quite matter-of-fact about it. "He has already resigned!"

"What!" The exclamation was an explosive, almost inarticulate sound. The scientist's large head hunched forward. "Say that again!"

"He has already resigned," came the quiet repetition, "but it has not yet taken effect. He is waiting, you see, to solve the problem of—er—myself. That finished, he is quite ready to turn the office of director over to his successor."

Bogert expelled his breath sharply. "And this successor? Who is he?" He was quite close to Herbie now, eyes fixed fascinatedly on those unreadable dull-red photoelectric cells that were the robot's eyes.

Words came slowly. "You are the next director."

And Bogert relaxed into a tight smile. "This is good to know. I've been hoping and waiting for this. Thanks, Herbie."

Peter Bogert was at his desk until five that morning, and he was back at nine. The shelf just over the desk emptied of its row of reference books and tables as he referred to one after the other. The pages of calculations before him increased microscopically, and the crumpled sheets at his feet mounted into a hill of scribbled paper.

At precisely noon he stared at the final page, rubbed a bloodshot eye, yawned and shrugged. "This is getting worse each minute. Damn!"

He turned at the sound of the opening door and nodded at Lanning, who entered, cracking the knuckles of one gnarled hand with the other.

The director took in the disorder of the room, and his eyebrows furrowed together.

"New lead?" he asked.

"No," came the defiant answer. "What's wrong with the old one?"

Lanning did not trouble to answer, nor to do more than bestow a single cursory glance at the top sheet upon Bogert's desk. He spoke through the flare of a match as he lit a cigar. "Has Calvin told you about the robot? It's a mathematical genius. Really remarkable."

The other snorted loudly. "So I've heard. But Calvin had better stick to robopsychology. I've checked Herbie on math, and he can scarcely struggle through calculus."

"Calvin didn't find it so."

"She's crazy."

"And I don't find it so." The director's eyes narrowed dangerously.

"You!" Bogert's voice hardened. "What are you talking about?"

"I've been putting Herbie through his paces all morning, and he can do tricks you never heard of."

"Is that so?"

"You sound skeptical!" Lanning flipped a sheet of paper out of his vest pocket and unfolded it. "That's not my handwriting, is it?"

10

Bogert studied the large angular notation covering the sheet. "Herbie did this?"

"Right! And if you'll notice, he's been working on your time integration of Equation 22. It comes"—Lanning tapped a yellow fingernail upon the last step—"to the identical conclusion I did, and in a quarter the time. You had no right to neglect the Linger Effect in positronic bombardment."

"I didn't neglect it. For heaven's sake, Lanning, get it through your head that it would cancel out—"

"Oh, sure, you explained that. You used the Mitchell Translation Equation, didn't you? Well—it doesn't apply."

"Why not?"

"Because you've been using hyperimaginaries, for one thing."

"What's that to do with?"

"Mitchell's equation won't hold when—"

"Are you crazy? If you'll reread Mitchell's original paper in the *Transactions of the Far*—"

"I don't have to. I told you in the beginning that I didn't like his reasoning, and Herbie backs me in that."

"Well, then," Bogert shouted, "let that clockwork contraption solve the entire problem for you. Why bother with nonessentials?"

"That's exactly the point. Herbie can't solve the problem. And if he can't, we can't—alone. I'm submitting the entire question to the National Board. It's gotten beyond us."

Bogert's chair went over backward as he jumped up asnarl, face crimson. "You're doing nothing of the sort."

Lanning flushed in his turn. "Are you telling me what I can't do?"

"Exactly," was the gritted response. "I've got the problem beaten and you're not to take it out of my hands, understand? Don't think I don't see through you, you desiccated fossil. You'd cut your own nose off before you'd let me get the credit for solving robotic telepathy."

"You're a damned idiot, Bogert, and in one second I'll have you suspended for insubordination." Lanning's lower lip trembled with passion.

"Which is one thing you won't do, Lanning. You haven't any secrets with a mind-reading robot around so don't forget that I know all about your resignation."

The ash on Lanning's cigar trembled and fell, and the cigar itself followed, "What . . . what—"

Bogert chuckled nastily. "And I'm the new director, be it understood. I'm very aware of that; don't think I'm not. Damn your eyes, Lanning, I'm going to give the orders about here or there will be the sweetest mess that you've ever been in."

Lanning found his voice and let it out with a roar. "You're suspended, d'ye hear? You're relieved of all duties. You're broken, do you understand?"

The smile on the other's face broadened. "Now, what's the use of that? You're getting nowhere. I'm holding the trumps. I know you've resigned. Herbie told me, and he got it straight from you."

Lanning forced himself to speak quietly. He looked an old, old man, with tired eyes peering from a face in which the red had disappeared, leaving the pasty yellow of age behind, "I want to speak to Herbie. He can't have told you anything of the sort. You're playing a deep game, Bogert, but I'm calling your bluff. Come with me."

Bogert shrugged. "To see Herbie? Good! Damned good!"

It was also precisely at noon that Milton Ashe looked up from his clumsy sketch and said, "You get the idea? I'm not too good at getting this down, but that's about how it looks. It's a honey of a house, and I can get it for next to nothing."

Susan Calvin gazed across at him with melting eyes. "It's really beautiful," she sighed. "I've often thought that I'd like to—" Her voice trailed away.

"Of course," Ashe continued briskly, putting away his pencil, "I've got to wait for my vacation. It's only two weeks off, but this Herbie business has everything up in the air." His eyes dropped to his fingernails. "Besides, there's another point—but it's a secret."

"Then don't tell me."

"Oh, I'd just as soon, I'm just busting to tell someone, and you're just about the best—er—confidante I could find here." He grinned sheepishly.

Susan Calvin's heart bounded, but she did not trust herself to speak.

"Frankly"—Ashe scraped his chair closer and lowered his voice into a confidential whisper—"the house isn't to be only for myself. I'm getting married!" And then he jumped out of his seat. "What's the matter?"

"Nothing!" The horrible spinning sensation had vanished, but it was hard to get words out. "Married? You mean—"

"Why, sure! About time, isn't it? You remember that girl who was here last summer. That's she! But you *are* sick. You—"

"Headache!" Susan Calvin motioned him away weakly. "I've . . . I've been subject to them lately. I want to . . . to congratulate you, of course. I'm very glad—" The inexpertly applied rouge made a pair of nasty splotches upon her chalk-white face. Things had begun spinning again. "Pardon me—please—"

The words were a mumble, as she stumbled blindly out the door. It had happened with the sudden catastrophe of a dream —and with all the unreal horror of a dream.

But how could it be? Herbie had said—

And Herbie knew! He could see into minds!

She found herself leaning breathlessly against the door jamb, staring into Herbie's metal face. She must have climbed the two flights of stairs, but she had no memory of it. The distance had been covered in an instant, as in a dream.

As in a dream!

And still Herbie's unblinking eyes stared into hers, and their dull red seemed to expand into dimly shining nightmarish globes.

He was speaking, and she felt the cold glass pressing against her lips. She swallowed and shuddered into a certain awareness of her surroundings.

Still Herbie spoke, and there was agitation in his voice—as if he were hurt and frightened and pleading.

The words were beginning to make sense. "This is a dream," he was saying, "and you mustn't believe in it. You'll wake into the real world soon and laugh at yourself. He loves you, I tell you. He does, he does! But not here! Not now! This is an illusion."

Susan Calvin nodded, her voice a whisper. "Yes! Yes!" She was clutching Herbie's arm, clinging to it, repeating over and over, "It isn't true, is it? It isn't, is it?"

Just how she came to her senses, she never knew—but it was like passing from a world of misty unreality to one of harsh sunlight. She pushed him away from her, pushed hard against that steely arm, and her eyes were wide.

"What are you trying to do?" Her voice rose to a harsh scream. "What are you trying to do?"

Herbie backed away. "I want to help."

The psychologist stared. "Help? By telling me this is a dream? By trying to push me into schizophrenia?" A hysterical tenseness seized her. "This is no dream! I wish it were!" She drew her breath sharply. "Wait! Why . . . why, I understand. Merciful heavens, it's so obvious."

There was horror in the robot's voice. "I had to!"

"And I believed you! I never thought—"

Loud voices outside the door brought her to a halt. She turned away, fists clenching spasmodically, and when Bogert and Lanning entered she was at the far window. Neither of the men paid her the slightest attention.

They approached Herbie simultaneously, Lanning angry and impatient, Bogert coolly sardonic. The director spoke first.

"Here, now, Herbie. Listen to me!"

The robot brought his eyes sharply down upon the aged director. "Yes, Dr. Lanning."

"Have you discussed me with Dr. Bogert?"

"No, sir." The answer came slowly, and the smile on Bogert's face flashed off.

"What's that?" Bogert shoved in ahead of his superior and straddled the ground before the robot. "Repeat what you told me yesterday."

"I said that—" Herbie fell silent. Deep within him his metallic diaphragm vibrated in soft discords.

"Didn't you say he had resigned?" roared Bogert. "Answer me!"

Bogert raised his arm frantically, but Lanning pushed him aside. "Are you trying to bully him into lying?"

"You heard him, Lanning. He began to say 'Yes' and stopped. Get out of my way! I want the truth out of him, understand!"

"I'll ask him!" Lanning turned to the robot. "All right, Herbie, take it easy. Have I resigned?"

Herbie stared, and Lanning repeated anxiously, "Have I resigned?" There was the faintest trace of a negative shake of the robot's head. A long wait produced nothing further.

The two men looked at each other, and the hostility in their eyes was all but tangible.

"What the devil," blurted Bogert, "has the robot gone mute? Can't you speak, you monstrosity?"

"I can speak," came the ready answer.

"Then answer the question. Didn't you tell me Lanning had resigned? Hasn't he resigned?"

And again there was nothing but dull silence, until from the end of the room, Susan Calvin's laugh rang out suddenly, high-pitched and semihysterical.

The two mathematicians jumped, and Bogert's eyes narrowed. "You here? What's so funny?"

"Nothing's funny." Her voice was not quite natural. "It's just that I'm not the only one that's been caught. There's irony in three of the greatest experts in robotics in the world falling into the same elementary trap, isn't there?" Her voice faded, and she put a pale hand to her forehead, "But it isn't funny!"

This time the look that passed between the two men was one of raised eyebrows. "What trap are you talking about?" asked Lanning stiffly. "Is something wrong with Herbie?"

"No." She approached them slowly. "Nothing is wrong with him—only with us." She whirled suddenly and shrieked at the robot, "Get away from me! Go to the other end of the room and don't let me look at you."

Herbie cringed before the fury of her eyes and stumbled away in a clattering trot.

Lanning's voice was hostile. "What is all this, Dr. Calvin?"

She faced them and spoke sarcastically. "Surely you know the fundamental First Law of Robotics."

The other two nodded together. "Certainly," said Bogert irritably. "A robot may not injure a human being or, through inaction, allow him to come to harm."

"How nicely put," sneered Calvin. "But what kind of harm?"

"Why—any kind."

"Exactly! Any kind! But what about hurt feelings? What about deflation of one's ego? What about the blasting of one's hopes? Is that injury?"

Lanning frowned. "What would a robot know about—" And then he caught himself with a gasp.

"You've caught on, have you? *This* robot reads minds. Do you suppose it doesn't know everything about mental injury?

Do you suppose that if asked a question it wouldn't give exactly that answer that one wants to hear? Wouldn't any other answer hurt us, and wouldn't Herbie know that?"

"Good heavens!" muttered Bogert.

The psychologist cast a sardonic glance at him. "I take it you asked him whether Lanning had resigned. You wanted to hear that he had resigned and so that's what Herbie told you."

"And I suppose that is why," said Lanning tonelessly, "it would not answer a little while ago. It couldn't answer either way without hurting one of us.

There was a short pause in which the men looked thoughtfully across the room at the robot, crouching in the chair by the bookcase, head resting in one hand.

Susan Calvin stared steadfastly at the floor. "He knew of all this. That . . . that devil knows everything—including what went wrong in his assembly." Her eyes were dark and brooding.

Lanning looked up. "You're wrong there, Dr. Calvin. He doesn't know what went wrong. I asked him."

"What does that mean?" cried Calvin. "Only that you didn't want him to give you the solution. It would puncture your ego to have a machine do what you couldn't. Did you ask him?" she shot at Bogert.

"In a way." Bogert coughed and reddened. "He told me he knew very little about mathematics."

Lanning laughed, not very loudly and the psychologist smiled caustically. She said, "I'll ask him! A solution by him won't hurt my ego." She raised her voice into a cold, imperative "Come here!"

Herbie rose and approached with hesitant steps.

"You know, I suppose," she continued, "just exactly at what point in the assembly an extraneous factor was introduced or an essential one left out."

"Yes," said Herbie, in tones barely heard.

"Hold on," broke in Bogert angrily. "That's not necessarily true. You want to hear that, that's all."

"Don't be a fool," replied Calvin. "He certainly knows as much math as you and Lanning together, since he can read minds. Give him his chance."

The mathematician subsided, and Calvin continued, "All right, then, Herbie, give! We're waiting." And in an aside, "Get pencils and paper, gentlemen."

But Herbie remained silent, and there was triumph in the psychologist's voice. "Why don't you answer, Herbie?"

The robot blurted out suddenly, "I cannot. You know I cannot! Dr. Bogert and Dr. Lanning don't want me to."

"They want the solution."

"But not from me."

Lanning broke in, speaking slowly and distinctly. "Don't be foolish, Herbie. We do want you to tell us."

Bogert nodded curtly.

Herbie's voice rose to wild heights. "What's the use of saying that? Don't you suppose that I can see past the superficial skin of your mind? Down below, you don't want me to. I'm a machine, given the imitation of life only by virtue of the positronic interplay in my brain—which is man's device. You can't lose face to me without being hurt. That is deep in your mind and won't be erased. I can't give the solution."

"We'll leave," said Dr. Lanning. "Tell Calvin."

"That would make no difference," cried Herbie, "since you would know anyway that it was I that was supplying the answer."

Calvin resumed, "But you understand, Herbie, that despite that, Doctors Lanning and Bogert want that solution."

"By their own efforts!" insisted Herbie.

"But they want it, and the fact that you have it and won't give it hurts them. You see that, don't you?"

"Yes! Yes!"

"And if you tell them that will hurt them, too."

"Yes! Yes!" Herbie was retreating slowly, and step by step Susan Calvin advanced. The two men watched in frozen bewilderment.

"You can't tell them," droned the psychologist slowly, "because that would hurt and you mustn't hurt. But if you don't tell them, you hurt, so you must tell them. And if you do, you will hurt and you mustn't, so you can't tell them; but if you don't you hurt, so you must; but if you do, you hurt, so you mustn't; but if you don't, you hurt, so you must; but if you do, you—"

Herbie was up against the wall, and here he dropped to his knees. "Stop!" he shrieked. "Close your mind! It is full of pain and frustration and hate! I didn't mean it, I tell you! I tried to help! I told you what you wanted to hear. I had to!"

The psychologist paid no attention. "You must tell them,

but if you do, you hurt, so you mustn't; but if you don't, you hurt, so you must; but—"

And Herbie screamed!

It was like the whistling of a piccolo many times magnified —shrill and shriller till it keened with the terror of a lost soul and filled the room with the piercingness of itself.

And when it died into nothingness, Herbie collapsed into a huddled heap of motionless metal.

Bogert's face was bloodless. "He's dead!"

"No!" Susan Calvin burst into body-racking gusts of wild laughter. "Not dead—merely insane. I confronted him with the insoluble dilemma, and he broke down. You can scrap him now—because he'll never speak again."

Lanning was on his knees beside the thing that had been Herbie. His fingers touched the cold, unresponsive metal face and he shuddered. "You did that on purpose." He rose and faced her, face contorted.

"What if I did? You can't help it now." And in a sudden access of bitterness: "He deserved it."

The director seized the paralyzed, motionless Bogert by the wrist. "What's the difference. Come, Peter." He sighed. "A thinking robot of this type is worthless, anyway." His eyes were old and tired, and he repeated, "Come, Peter!"

It was minutes after the two scientists left that Dr. Susan Calvin regained part of her mental equilibrium. Slowly her eyes turned to the living-dead Herbie, and the tightness returned to her face. Long she stared while the triumph faded and the helpless frustration returned—and of all her turbulent thoughts only one infinitely bitter word passed her lips:

"Liar!"

It's a *Good* Life

JEROME BIXBY

This is one of the most frightening stories I've ever read. Jerry Bixby, enthusiastic piano-pounder, former editor, West Coast denizen, and all-around good fellow, has never written anything else quite like it. I went around wondering for days after I read it, and I shouldn't be at all surprised if you did. But, after all, it's only a story.
I hope.

Aunt Amy was out on the front porch, rocking back and forth in the high-backed chair and fanning herself, when Bill Soames rode his bicycle up the road and stopped in front of the house.

Perspiring under the afternoon "sun," Bill lifted the box of groceries out of the big basket over the front wheel of the bike and came up the front walk.

Little Anthony was sitting on the lawn, playing with a rat. He had caught the rat down in the basement—he had made it think that it smelled cheese, the most rich-smelling and crumbly-delicious cheese a rat had ever thought it smelled, and it had come out of its hole, and now Anthony had hold of it with his mind and was making it do tricks.

When the rat saw Bill Soames coming, it tried to run, but Anthony thought at it, and it turned a flip-flop on the grass and lay trembling, its eyes gleaming in small black terror.

Bill Soames hurried past Anthony and reached the front steps, mumbling. He always mumbled when he came to the Fremont house, or passed by it, or even thought of it. Everybody did. They thought about silly things, things that didn't mean very much, like two-and-two-is-four-and-twice-is-eight and so on; they tried to jumble up their thoughts and keep them skipping back and forth, so Anthony couldn't read their minds. The mumbling helped. Because if Anthony got any-

19

thing strong out of your thoughts, he might take a notion to do something about it—like curing your wife's sick headaches or your kid's mumps, or getting your old milk cow back on schedule, or fixing the privy. And while Anthony mightn't actually mean any harm, he couldn't be expected to have much notion of what was the right thing to do in such cases.

That was if he liked you. He might try to help you, in his way. And that could be pretty horrible.

If he didn't like you—well, that could be worse.

Bill Soames set the box of groceries on the porch railing and stopped his mumbling long enough to say, "Everythin' you wanted, Miss Amy."

"Oh, fine, William," Amy Fremont said lightly. "My, ain't it terrible hot today?"

Bill Soames almost cringed. His eyes pleaded with her. He shook his head violently *no,* and then interrupted his mumbling again, though obviously he didn't want to. "Oh, don't say that, Miss Amy. It's fine, just fine. A real *good* day!"

Amy Fremont got up from the rocking chair and came across the porch. She was a tall woman, thin, a smiling vacancy in her eyes. About a year ago Anthony had got mad at her, because she'd told him he shouldn't have turned the cat into a cat rug, and although he had always obeyed her more than anyone else, which was hardly at all, this time he'd snapped at her. With his mind. And that had been the end of Amy Fremont's bright eyes, and the end of Amy Fremont as everyone had known her. And that was when word got around in Peaksville (population forty-six) that even the members of Anthony's own family weren't safe. After that, everyone was twice as careful.

Someday Anthony might undo what he'd done to Aunt Amy. Anthony's Mom and Pop hoped he would. When he was older, and maybe sorry. If it was possible, that is. Because Aunt Amy had changed a lot, and besides, now Anthony wouldn't obey anyone.

"Land alive, William," Aunt Amy said, "you don't have to mumble like that. Anthony wouldn't hurt you. My goodness, Anthony likes you!" She raised her voice and called to Anthony, who had tired of the rat and was making it eat itself, "Don't you, dear? Don't you like Mr. Soames?"

Anthony looked across the lawn at the grocery man—a

bright, wet, purple gaze. He didn't say anything. Bill Soames tried to smile at him. After a second Anthony returned his attention to the rat. It had already devoured its tail, or at least chewed it off—for Anthony had made it bite faster than it could swallow, and little pink and red furry pieces lay around it on the green grass. Now the rat was having trouble reaching its hindquarters.

Mumbling silently, thinking of nothing in particular as hard as he could, Bill Soames went stiff-legged down the walk, mounted his bicycle and pedaled off.

"We'll see you tonight, William," Aunt Amy called after him.

As Bill Soames pumped the pedals, he was wishing deep down that he could pump twice as fast, to get away from Anthony all the faster, and away from Aunt Amy, who sometimes just forgot how *careful* you had to be. And he shouldn't have thought that. Because Anthony caught it. He caught the desire to get away from the Fremont house as if it was something *bad,* and his purple gaze blinked, and he snapped a small, sulky thought after Bill Soames—just a small one, because he was in a good mood today, and besides, he liked Bill Soames, or at least didn't dislike him, at least today. Bill Soames wanted to go away—so, petulantly, Anthoy helped him.

Pedaling with superhuman speed—or, rather, appearing to, because in reality the bicycle was pedaling *him*—Bill Soames vanished down the road in a cloud of dust, his thin, terrified wail drifting back across the summerlike heat.

Anthony looked at the rat. It had devoured half its belly, and had died from pain. He thought it into a grave out deep in the cornfield—his father had once said, smiling, that he might as well do that with the things he killed—and went around the house, casting his odd shadow in the hot, brassy light from above.

In the kitchen, Aunt Amy was unpacking the groceries. She put the Mason-jarred goods on the shelves, and the meat and milk in the icebox, and the beet sugar and coarse flour in big cans under the sink. She put the cardboard box in the corner, by the door, for Mr. Soames to pick up next time he came. It was stained and battered and torn and worn fuzzy, but it was one of the few left in Peaksville. In faded red letters it said "Campbell's Soup." The last cans of soup, or of anything else, had been eaten long ago, except for a small communal hoard which the villagers dipped into for special occasions—but the box lingered on, like a coffin, and when it and the other boxes were gone the men would have to make some out of wood.

Aunt Amy went out in back, where Anthony's Mom— Aunt Amy's sister—sat in the shade of the house, shelling peas. The peas, every time Mom ran a finger along a pod, went *lollop-lollop-lollop* into the pan on her lap.

"William brought the groceries," Aunt Amy said. She sat down wearily in the straight-backed chair beside Mom and began fanning herself again. She wasn't really old; but ever since Anthony had snapped at her with his mind, something had seemed to be wrong with her body as well as her mind, and she was tired all the time.

"Oh, good," said Mom. *Lollop* went the fat peas into the pan.

Everybody in Peaksville always said, "Oh, fine," or "Good," or "Say, that's swell!" when almost anything happened or was mentioned—even unhappy things like accidents or even deaths. They'd always say "Good" because if they didn't try to cover up how they really felt Anthony might overhear with his mind, and then nobody knew what might happen. Like the time Mrs. Kent's husband, Sam, had come walking back from the graveyard because Anthony liked Mrs. Kent and had heard her mourning.

Lollop.

"Tonight's television night," said Aunt Amy. "I'm glad. I look forward to it so much every week. I wonder what we'll see tonight."

"Did Bill bring the meat?" asked Mom.

"Yes." Aunt Amy fanned herself, looking up at the featureless brassy glare of the sky. "Goodness, it's so hot! I wish Anthony would make it just a little cooler—"

"*Amy!*"

"Oh!" Mom's sharp tone had penetrated where Bill Soames's agonized expression had failed. Aunt Amy put one thin hand to her mouth in exaggerated alarm. "Oh . . . I'm sorry, dear." Her pale-blue eyes shuttled around, right and left, to see if Anthony was in sight. Not that it would make any difference if he was or wasn't—he didn't have to be near you to know what you were thinking. Usually, though, unless he had his attention on somebody, he would be occupied with thoughts of his own.

But some things attracted his attention—you could never be sure just what.

"This weather's just *fine*," Mom said.

Lollop.

"Oh, yes," Aunt Amy said. "It's a wonderful day. I wouldn't want it changed for the world!"

Lollop.

Lollop.

"What time is it?" Mom asked.

Aunt Amy was sitting where she could see through the kitchen window to the alarm clock on the shelf above the stove. "Four-thirty," she said.

Lollop.

"I want tonight to be something special," Mom said. "Did Bill bring a good lean roast?"

"Good and lean, dear. They butchered just today, you know, and sent us over the best piece."

"Dan Hollis will be *so* surprised when he finds out that tonight's television party is a birthday party for him, too!"

"Oh *I* think he will! Are you sure nobody's told him?"

"Everybody swore they wouldn't."

"That'll be real nice." Aunt Amy nodded, looking off across the cornfield. "A birthday party."

"Well—" Mom put the pan of peas down beside her, stood up and brushed her apron—"I'd better get the roast on. Then we can set the table." She picked up the peas.

Anthony came around the corner of the house. He didn't look at them, but continued on down through the carefully kept garden—*all* the gardens in Peaksville were carefully kept, very carefully kept—and went past the rustling, useless hulk that had been the Fremont family car, and went smoothly over the fence and out into the cornfield.

"Isn't this a lovely day!" said Mom, a little loudly, as they went toward the back door.

Aunt Amy fanned herself. "A beautiful day, dear. Just *fine!*"

Out in the cornfield, Anthony walked between the tall, rustling rows of green stalks. He liked to smell the corn. The alive corn overhead, and the old dead corn underfoot. Rich Ohio earth, thick with weeds and brown, dry-rotting ears of corn, pressed between his bare toes with every step—he had made it rain last night so everything would smell and feel nice today.

He walked clear to the edge of the cornfield, and over to where a grove of shadowy green trees covered cool, moist, dark ground and lots of leafy undergrowth and jumbled moss-covered rocks and a small spring that made a clear, clean pool. Here Anthony liked to rest and watch the birds and insects and small animals that rustled and scampered and chirped about. He liked to lie on the cool ground and look up through the moving greenness overhead and watch the insects flit in the hazy soft sunbeams that stood like slanting, glowing bars between ground and treetops. Somehow, he liked the thoughts of the little creatures in this place better than the thoughts outside; and while the thoughts he picked up here weren't very strong or very clear, he could get enough out of them to know what the little creatures liked and wanted, and he spent a lot of time making the grove more like what they wanted it to be. The spring hadn't always been here; but one time he had found thirst in one small furry mind, and had brought subterranean water to the surface in a clear cold flow and had watched, blinking, as the creature drank, feeling its pleasure. Later he had made the pool, when he found a small urge to swim.

He had made rocks and trees and bushes and caves, and sunlight here and shadows there, because he had felt in all the tiny minds around him the desire—or the instinctive want —for this kind of resting place, and that kind of mating place, and this kind of place to play, and that kind of home. And somehow the creatures from all the fields and pastures around the grove had seemed to know that this was a good place, for there were always more of them coming in. Every time Anthony came out here there were more creatures than the last time, and more desires and needs to be tended to. Every time there would be some kind of creature he had never seen before, and he would find its mind, and see what it wanted, and then give it to it. He liked to help them. He liked to feel their simple gratification.

Today he rested beneath a thick elm and lifted his purple gaze to a red-and-black bird that had just come to the grove. It twittered on a branch over his head, and hopped back and forth, and thought its tiny thoughts, and Anthony made a big, soft nest for it, and pretty soon it hopped in.

A long brown, sleek-furred animal was drinking at the pool. Anthony found its mind next. The animal was thinking about a smaller creature that was scurrying along the ground on the other side of the pool, grubbing for insects. The little creature didn't know it was in danger. The long brown animal finished drinking and tensed its legs to leap, and Anthony thought it into a grave in the cornfield.

He didn't like those kinds of thoughts. They reminded him of the thoughts outside the grove. A long time ago some of the people outside had thought that way about *him*, and one night they'd hidden and waited for him to come back from the grove—and he'd just thought them all into the cornfield. Since then the rest of the people hadn't thought that way— at least, very clearly. Now their thoughts were all mixed up and confusing whenever they thought about him or near him, so he didn't pay much attention.

He liked to help them too, sometimes—but it wasn't simple, or very gratifying either. They never thought happy thoughts when he did—just the jumble. So he spent more time out here.

He watched all the birds and insects and furry creatures for a while, and played with a bird, making it soar and dip and streak madly around tree trunks until, accidentally, when another bird caught his attention for a moment, he ran it into a rock. Petulantly, he thought the rock into a grave in the cornfield; but he couldn't do anything more with the bird. Not because it was dead, though it was; but because it had a broken wing. So he went back to the house. He didn't feel like walking back through the cornfield, so he just *went* to the house, right down into the basement.

It was nice down here. Nice and dark and damp and sort of fragrant, because once Mom had been making preserves in a rack along the far wall and then she'd stopped coming down ever since Anthony had started spending time here, and the preserves had spoiled and leaked down and spread over the dirt floor and Anthony liked the smell.

He caught another rat, making it smell cheese, and after he played with it he thought it into a grave right beside the long animal he'd killed in the grove. Aunt Amy hated rats, and so he killed a lot of them, because he liked Aunt Amy most of all and sometimes did things Aunt Amy wanted. Her mind was more like the little furry minds out in the grove. She hadn't thought anything bad at all about him for a long time.

After the rat, he played with a big black spider in the corner under the stairs, making it run back and forth until its web shook and shimmered in the light from the cellar window like a reflection in silvery water. Then he drove fruit flies into the web until the spider was frantic trying to wind them all up. The spider liked flies, and its thoughts were stronger than theirs, so he did it. There was something bad in the way it liked flies, but it wasn't clear—and besides, Aunt Amy hated flies too.

He heard footsteps overhead—Mom moving around in the kitchen. He blinked his purple gaze and almost decided to make her hold still—but instead he went up to the attic, and, after looking out the circular window for a while at the front lawn and the dusty road and Henderson's tip-waving wheatfield beyond, he curled into an unlikely shape and went partly to sleep.

Soon people would be coming for television, he heard Mom think.

He went more to sleep. He liked television night. Aunt Amy had always liked television a lot, so one time he had thought some for her, and a few other people had been there at the time, and Aunt Amy had felt disappointed when they wanted to leave. He'd done something to them for that —and now everybody came to television.

He liked all the attention he got when they did.

Anthony's father came home around six-thirty, looking tired and dirty and bloody. He'd been over in Dunn's pasture with the other men, helping pick out the cow to be slaughtered this month, and doing the job, and then butchering the meat and salting it away in Soames's icehouse. Not a job he cared for, but every man had his turn. Yesterday he had helped scythe down old McIntyre's wheat. Tomorrow they would start threshing. By hand. Everything in Peaksville had to be done by hand.

He kissed his wife on the cheek and sat down at the kitchen table. He smiled and said, "Where's Anthony?"

"Around someplace," Mom said.

Aunt Amy was over at the wood-burning stove, stirring the big pot of peas. Mom went back to the oven and opened it and basted the roast.

"Well, it's been a *good* day," Dad said. By rote. Then he looked at the mixing bowl and breadboard on the table. He sniffed at the dough. "M'm," he said. "I could eat a loaf all by myself, I'm so hungry."

"No one told Dan Hollis about its being a birthday party, did they?" his wife asked.

"Nope. We kept as quiet as mummies."

"We've fixed up such a lovely surprise!"

"Um? What?"

"Well . . . you know how much Dan likes music. Well, last week Thelma Dunn found a *record* in her attic!"

"No!"

"Yes! And we had Ethel sort of ask—you know, without really *asking*—if he had that one. And he said no. Isn't that a wonderful surprise?"

"Well, now, it sure is. A record, imagine! That's a real nice thing to find! What record is it?"

"Perry Como, singing 'You Are My Sunshine.' "

"Well, I'll be darned. I always liked that tune." Some raw carrots were lying on the table. Dad picked up a small one, scrubbed it on his chest, and took a bite. "How did Thelma happen to find it?"

"Oh, you know—just looking around for new things."

"M'm." Dad chewed the carrot. "Say, who has that picture we found a while back? I kind of liked it—that old clipper sailing along . . ."

"The Smiths. Next week the Sipiches get it, and they give the Smiths old McIntyre's music-box, and we give the Sipiches . . ." And she went down the tentative order of things that would exchange hands among the women at church this Sunday.

He nodded. "Looks like we can't have the picture for a while, I guess. Look, honey, you might try to get that detective book back from the Reillys. I was so busy the week we had it, I never got to finish all the stories."

"I'll try," his wife said doubtfully. "But I hear the Van Husens have a stereoscope they found in the cellar." Her voice was just a little accusing. "They had it two whole months before they told anybody about it."

"Say," Dad said, looking interested, "that'd be nice, too. Lots of pictures?"

"I suppose so. I'll see on Sunday. I'd like to have it—but we still owe the Van Husens for their canary. I don't know why that bird had to pick *our* house to die—it must have been sick when we got it. Now there's just no satisfying Betty Van Husen. She even hinted she'd like our *piano* for a while!"

"Well, honey, you try for the stereoscope—or just anything you think we'll like." At last he swallowed the carrot. It had been a little young and tough. Anthony's whims about the weather made it so that people never knew what crops would come up, or what shape they'd be in if they did. All they could do was plant a lot; and always enough of something came up any one season to live on. Just once there had been a grain surplus; tons of it had been hauled to the edge of Peaksville and dumped off into the nothingness. Otherwise, nobody could have breathed when it started to spoil.

"You know," Dad went on, "it's nice to have the new things around. It's nice to think that there's probably still a lot of stuff nobody's found yet, in cellars and attics and barns and down behind things. They help, somehow. As much as anything can help—"

"Sh-h!" Mom glanced nervously around.

"Oh," Dad said, smiling hastily, "it's all right! The new things are *good!* It's *nice* to be able to have something around you've never seen before, and know that something you've given somebody else is making them happy. That's a real *good* thing."

"A good thing," his wife echoed.

"Pretty soon," Aunt Amy said, from the stove, "there won't be any more new things. We'll have found everything there is to find. Goodness, that'll to be too bad."

"*Amy!*"

"Well . . ." Her pale eyes were shallow and fixed, a sign of her recurrent vagueness. "It will be kind of a shame—no new things—"

"Don't *talk* like that," Mom said, trembling. "Amy, be *quiet!*"

"It's *good*," said Dad, in the loud, familiar, wanting-to-be-overheard tone of voice. "Such talk is *good*. It's okay, honey

—don't you see? It's good for Amy to talk any way she wants. It's good for her to feel bad. Everything's good. Everything *has* to be good."

Anthony's mother was pale. And so was Aunt Amy—the peril of the moment had suddenly penetrated the clouds surrounding her mind. Sometimes it was difficult to handle words so that they might not prove disastrous. You just never *knew*. There were so many things it was wise not to say, or even think—but remonstration for saying or thinking them might be just as bad, if Anthony heard and decided to do anything about it. You could just never tell what Anthony was liable to do.

Everything had to be good. Had to be fine just as it was, even if it wasn't. Always. Because any change might be worse. So terribly much worse.

"Oh, my goodness, yes, of course it's good," Mom said. "You talk any way you want to, Amy, and it's just fine. Of course, you want to remember that some ways are *better* than others."

Aunt Amy stirred the peas, fright in her pale eyes.

"Oh, yes," she said. "But I don't feel like talking right now. It . . . it's *good* that I don't feel like talking."

Dad said tiredly, smiling, "I'm going out and wash up."

They started arriving around eight o'clock. By that time Mom and Aunt Amy had the big table in the dining room set, and two more tables off to the side. The candles were burning, and the chairs situated, and Dad had a big fire going in the fireplace.

The first to arrive were the Sipiches, John and Mary. John wore his best suit, and was well scrubbed and pink-faced after his day in McIntyre's pasture. The suit was neatly pressed but getting threadbare at elbows and cuffs. Old McIntyre was working on a loom, designing it out of schoolbooks, but so far it was slow going. McIntyre was a capable man with wood and tools, but a loom was a big order when you couldn't get metal parts. McIntyre had been one of the ones who, at first, had wanted to try to get Anthony to make things the villagers needed, like clothes and canned goods and medical supplies and gasoline. Since then he felt that what had happened to the whole Terrance family and Joe Kinney was his fault, and he worked hard trying to make it up to the rest of them. And since then no one had tried to get Anthony to do anything.

Mary Sipich was a small, cheerful woman in a simple dress. She immediately set about helping Mom and Aunt Amy put the finishing touches on the dinner.

The next arrivals were the Smiths and the Dunns, who lived right next to each other down the road, only a few yards from the nothingness. They drove up in the Smiths' wagon, drawn by their old horse.

Then the Reilly's showed up, from across the darkened wheatfield, and the evening really began. Pat Reilly sat down at the big upright in the front room and began to play from the popular sheet music on the rack. He played softly, as expressively as he could—and nobody sang. Anthony liked piano playing a whole lot, but not singing; often he would come up from the basement, or down from the attic, or just *come*, and sit on top of the piano, nodding his head as Pat played "Lover" or "Boulevard of Broken Dreams" or "Night and Day." He seemed to prefer ballads, sweet-sounding songs —but the one time somebody had started to sing, Anthony had looked over from the top of the piano and done something that made everybody afraid of singing from then on. Later they'd decided that the piano was what Anthony had heard first, before anybody had ever tried to sing, and now anything else added to it didn't sound right and distracted him from his pleasure.

So every television night Pat would play the piano, and that was the beginning of the evening. Wherever Anthony was, the music would make him happy and put him in a good mood, and he would know that they were gathering for television and waiting for him.

By eight-thirty everybody had shown up, except for the seventeen children and Mrs. Soames, who was off watching them in the schoolhouse at the far end of town. The children of Peaksville were never, never, allowed near the Fremont house—not since little Fred Smith had tried to play with Anthony on a dare. The younger children weren't even told about Anthony. The others had mostly forgotten about him, or were told that he was a nice, nice goblin but they must never go near him.

Dan and Ethel Hollis came late, and Dan walked in not

suspecting a thing. Pat Reilly had played the piano until his hands ached—he'd worked pretty hard with them today—and now he got up, and everybody gathered around to wish Dan Hollis a happy birthday.

"Well, I'll be darned," Dan grinned. "This is swell. I wasn't expecting this at all . . . gosh, this is *swell!*"

They gave him his presents—mostly things they had made by hand, though some were things that people had possessed as their own and now gave him as his. John Sipich gave him a watch charm, hand-carved out of a piece of hickory wood. Dan's watch had broken down a year or so ago, and there was nobody in the village who knew how to fix it, but he still carried it around because it had been his grandfather's and was a fine old heavy thing of gold and silver. He attached the charm to the chain while everybody laughed and said John had done a nice job of carving. Then Mary Sipich gave him a knitted necktie, which he put on, removing the one he'd worn.

The Reillys gave him a little box they had made, to keep things in. They didn't say what things, but Dan said he'd keep his personal jewelry in it. The Reillys had made it out of a cigar box, carefully peeled of its paper and lined on the inside with velvet. The outside had been polished, and carefully if not expertly carved by Pat—but his carving got complimented, too. Dan Hollis received many other gifts—a pipe, a pair of shoelaces, a tiepin, a knit pair of socks, some fudge, a pair of garters made from old suspenders.

He unwrapped each gift with vast pleasure and wore as many of them as he could right there, even the garters. He lit up the pipe and said he'd never had a better smoke. Which wasn't quite true, because the pipe wasn't broken in yet; Pete Manners had had it lying around ever since he'd received it as a gift four years ago from an out-of-town relative who hadn't known he'd stopped smoking.

Dan put the tobacco into the bowl very carefully. Tobacco was precious. It was only pure luck that Pat Reilly had decided to try to grow some in his back yard just before what had happened to Peaksville had happened. It didn't grow very well, and then they had to cure it and shred it and all, and it was just precious stuff. Everybody in town used wooden holders old McIntyre had made, to save on butts.

Last of all, Thelma Dunn gave Dan Hollis the record she had found.

Dan's eyes misted even before he opened the package. He knew it was a record.

"Gosh," he said softly. "What one is it? I'm almost afraid to look . . ."

"You haven't got it, darling," Ethel Hollis smiled. "Don't you remember, I asked about 'You Are My Sunshine'?"

"Oh, gosh," Dan said again. Carefully he removed the wrapping and stood there fondling the record, running his big hands over the worn grooves with their tiny, dulling crosswise scratches. He looked around the room, eyes shining, and they all smiled back, knowing how delighted he was.

"Happy birthday, darling!" Ethel said, throwing her arms around him and kissing him.

He clutched the record in both hands, holding it off to one side as she pressed against him. "Hey," he laughed, pulling back his head. "Be careful—I'm holding a priceless object!" He looked around again, over his wife's arms, which were still around his neck. His eyes were hungry. "Look . . . do you think we could play it? Lord, what I'd give to hear some new music. Just the first part, the orchestra part, before Como sings?"

Faces sobered. After a minute, John Sipich said, "I don't think we'd better, Dan. After all, we don't know just where the singer comes in—it'd be taking too much of a chance. Better wait till you get home."

Dan Hollis reluctantly put the record on the buffet with all his other presents. "It's *good*," he said automatically, but disappointedly, "that I can't play it here."

"Oh, yes," said Sipich. "It's good." To compensate for Dan's disappointed tone, he repeated, "It's *good*."

They ate dinner, the candles lighting their smiling faces, and ate it all right down to the last delicious drop of gravy. They complimented Mom and Aunt Amy on the roast beef, and the peas and carrots, and the tender corn on the cob. The corn hadn't come from the Fremonts' cornfield, naturally—everybody knew what was out there, and the field was going to weeds. Then they polished off the dessert—homemade ice cream and cookies. And then they sat back, in the flickering light of the candles, and chatted, waiting for television.

There never was a lot of mumbling on television night—

everybody came and had a good dinner at the Fremonts', and that was nice, and afterward there was television, and nobody really thought much about that—it just had to be put up with. So it was a pleasant enough get-together, aside from your having to watch what you said just as carefully as you always did everyplace. If a dangerous thought came into your mind, you just started mumbling, even right in the middle of a sentence. When you did that, the others just ignored you until you felt happier again and stopped.

Anthony liked television night. He had done only two or three awful things on television night in the whole past year.

Mom had put a bottle of brandy on the table, and they each had a tiny glass of it. Liquor was even more precious than tobacco. The villagers could make wine, but the grapes weren't right, and certainly the techniques weren't, and it wasn't very good wine. There were only a few bottles of real liquor left in the village—four rye, three Scotch, three brandy, nine real wine and half a bottle of Drambuie belonging to old McIntyre (only for marriages)—and when those were gone, that was it.

Afterward everybody wished that the brandy hadn't been brought out. Because Dan Hollis drank more of it than he should have, and mixed it with a lot of the homemade wine. Nobody thought anything about it at first, because he didn't show it much outside, and it was his birthday party and a happy party, and Anthony liked these get-togethers and shouldn't see any reason to do anything even if he was listening. But Dan Hollis got high, and did a fool thing. If they'd seen it coming, they'd have taken him outside and walked him around.

The first thing they knew, Dan stopped laughing right in the middle of the story about how Thelma Dunn had found the Perry Como record and dropped it and it hadn't broken because she'd moved faster than she ever had before in her life and caught it. He was fondling the record again, and looking longingly at the Fremonts' gramophone over in the corner, and suddenly he stopped laughing and his face got slack, and then it got ugly, and he said, "Oh, *Christ!*"

Immediately the room was still. So still they could hear the whirring movement of the grandfather's clock out in the hall. Pat Reilly had been playing the piano, softly. He stopped, his hands poised over the yellowed keys.

The candles on the dining-room table flickered in a cool

breeze that blew through the lace curtains over the bay window.

"Keep playing, Pat," Anthony's father said softly.

Pat started again. He played "Night and Day," but his eyes were sidewise on Dan Hollis, and he missed notes.

Dan stood in the middle of the room, holding the record. In his other hand he held a glass of brandy so hard his hand shook.

They were all looking at him.

"*Christ,*" he said again, and he made it sound like a dirty word.

Reverend Younger, who had been talking with Mom and Aunt Amy by the dining-room door, said "Christ," too—but he was using it in a prayer. His hands were clasped, and his eyes were closed.

John Sipich moved forward. "Now, Dan. It's *good* for you to talk that way, but you don't want to talk too much, you know."

Dan shook off the hand Sipich put on his arm.

"Can't even play my record," he said loudly. He looked down at the record, and then around at their faces. "Oh, my *God*—" He threw the glassful of brandy against the wall. It splattered and ran down the wallpaper in streaks.

Some of the women gasped.

"Dan," Sipich said in a whisper. "Dan, cut it out."

Pat Reilly was playing "Night and Day" louder, to cover up the sounds of the talk. It wouldn't do any good, though, if Anthony was listening. Dan Hollis went over to the piano and stood by Pat's shoulder, swaying a little. "Pat," he said, "don't play *that*. Play *this*." And he began to sing, softly, hoarsely, miserably, "Happy birthday to me, happy birthday to me . . ."

"*Dan!*" Ethel Hollis screamed. She tried to run across the room to him. Mary Sipich grabbed her arm and held her back. "Dan," Ethel screamed again, "stop—"

"My God, be quiet!" hissed Mary Sipich, and pushed her toward one of the men, who put his hand over her mouth and held her still.

". . . happy birthday, dear Danny," Dan sang, "happy birthday to me!" He stopped and looked down at Pat Reilly. "Play it, Pat. Play it, so I can sing right. You know I can't carry a tune unless somebody plays it!"

Pat Reilly put his hands on the keys and began "Lover"—in

a slow waltz tempo, the way Anthony like it. Pat's face was white. His hands fumbled.

Dan Hollis stared over at the dining-room door. At Anthony's mother, and at Anthony's father, who had gone to join her. "*You* had him," he said. Tears gleamed on his cheeks as the candlelight caught them. "*You* had to go and *have* him . . ." He closed his eyes, and the tears squeezed out. He sang loudly, "You are my sunshine . . . my only sunshine . . . you make me happy . . . when I am blue . . ."

Anthony came into the room.

Pat stopped playing. He froze. Everybody froze. The breeze rippled the curtains. Ethel Hollis couldn't even try to scream— she had fainted.

". . . please don't take my sunshine . . . away . . ." Dan's voice faltered into silence. His eyes widened. He put both hands out in front of him, the empty glass in one, the record in the other. He hiccuped and said, *"No—"*

"Bad man," Anthony said, and thought Dan Hollis into something like nothing anyone would have believed possible, and then he thought the thing into a grave deep, deep in the cornfield.

The glass and the record thumped on the rug. Neither broke.

Anthony's purple gaze went around the room.

Some of the people began mumbling. They all tried to smile. The sound of mumbling filled the room like a far-off approval. Out of the murmuring came one or two clear voices:

"Oh, it's a very *good* thing," said John Sipich.

"A good thing," said Anthony's father, smiling. He'd had more practice in smiling than most of them. "A wonderful thing."

"It's swell . . . just swell," said Pat Reilly, tears leaking from eyes and nose, and he began to play the piano again, softly, his trembling hands feeling for "Night and Day."

Anthony cilmbed up on top of the piano, and Pat played for two hours.

Afterward, they watched television. They all went into the front room, and lit just a few candles, and pulled up chairs around the set. It was a small-screen set, and they couldn't all sit close enough to it to see, but that didn't matter. They didn't even turn the set on. It wouldn't have worked anyway, there being no electricity in Peaksville.

They just sat silently, and watched the twisting, writhing

shapes on the screen, and listened to the sounds that came out of the speaker, and none of them had any idea of what it was all about. They never did. It was always the same.

"It's real nice," Aunt Amy said once, her pale eyes on the meaningless flickers and shadows. "But I liked it a little better when there were cities outside and we could get real—"

"Why, Amy!" said Mom. "It's good for you to say such a thing. Very good. But how can you mean it? Why, this television is *much* better than anything we ever used to get!"

"Yes," chimed in John Sipich. "It's fine. It's the best show we've ever seen!"

He sat on the couch with two other men, holding Ethel Hollis flat against the cushions, holding her arms and legs and putting their hands over her mouth so she couldn't start screaming again.

"It's really *good!*" he said again.

Mom looked out of the front window, across the darkened road, across Henderson's darkened wheat field to the vast, endless gray nothingness in which the little village of Peaksville floated like a soul—the huge nothingness that was most evident at night, when Anthony's brassy day had gone.

It did no good to wonder where they were—no good at all. Peaksville was just someplace. Someplace away from the world. It was wherever it had been since that day three years ago when Anthony had crept from her womb and old Doc Bates—God rest him—had screamed and dropped him and tried to kill him, and Anthony had whined and done the thing. Had taken the village someplace. Or had destroyed the world and left only the village, nobody knew which.

It did no good to wonder about it. Nothing at all did any good—except to live as they must live. Must always, always live, if Anthony would let them.

These thoughts were dangerous, she thought.

She began to mumble. The others started mumbling, too. They had all been thinking, evidently.

The men on the couch whispered and whispered to Ethel Hollis, and when they took their hands away she mumbled, too.

While Anthony sat on top of the set and made television, they sat around and mumbled and watched the meaningless, flickering shapes far into the night.

Next day it snowed, and killed off half the crops—but it was a *good* day.

The Veldt

RAY BRADBURY

It is very clear that if this anthology had been begun ten years ago Ray Bradbury would have received a great many more than four votes. The fashion began to change, as nearly as I can see, when it was discovered that Mr. Bradbury either could not write like or had no interest in writing like Heinlein, Campbell, Wells or, for that matter, John O'Hara. This, for some reason, seemed to irritate people.

Mr. Bradbury, meanwhile, has simply continued to write like Bradbury, an enviable thing to be able to do. I don't think we have the right to ask for more than this, and I, for one, really don't want to. While such a mythical reshifting took place, we might miss another story as good as this one.

The original appearance of "The Veldt" in The Saturday Evening Post must have turned a number of normally cheerful suburbanites the color of their own lawns. Don't say you weren't warned.

"George, I wish you'd look at the nursery."

"What's wrong with it?"

"I don't know."

"Well, then."

"I just want you to look at it, is all, or call a psychologist in to look at it."

"What would a psychologist want with a nursery?"

"You know very well what he'd want." His wife paused in the middle of the kitchen and watched the stove busy humming to itself, making supper for four. "It's just that the nursery is different now than it was."

"All right, let's have a look."

They walked down the hall of their soundproofed Happy-Life Home, which had cost them thirty thousand dollars installed, this house which clothed and fed them and rocked them to sleep and played and sang and was good to them. Their approach sensitized a switch somewhere and the nursery light flicked on when they came within ten feet of it. Similarly, behind them, in the halls, lights went on and off as they left them behind, with a soft automaticity.

"Well," said George Hadley.

They stood on the thatched floor of the nursery. It was forty feet across by forty feet long and thirty feet high; it had cost half again as much as the rest of the house. "But nothing's too good for our children," George had said.

The nursery was silent. It was empty as a jungle glade at hot high noon. The walls were blank and two-dimensional. Now, as George and Lydia Hadley stood in the center of the room, the walls began to purr and recede into crystalline distance, it seemed, and presently an African veldt appeared, in three dimensions; on all sides, in colors reproduced to the final pebble and bit of straw. The ceiling above them became a deep sky with a hot yellow sun.

George Hadley felt the perspiration start on his brow.

"Let's get out of the sun," he said. "This is a little too real. But I don't see anything wrong."

"Wait a moment, you'll see," said his wife.

Now the hidden odorophonics were beginning to blow a wind of odor at the two people in the middle of the baked veldtland. The hot straw smell of lion grass, the cool green smell of the hidden water hole, the great rusty smell of animals, the smell of dust like a red paprika in the hot air. And now the sounds: the thump of distant antelope feet on grassy sod, the papery rustling of vultures. A shadow passed through the sky. The shadow flickered on George Hadley's upturned, sweating face.

"Filthy creatures," he heard his wife say.

"The vultures."

"You see, there are the lions, far over, that way. Now they're on their way to the water hole. They've just been eating," said Lydia. "I don't know what."

"Some animal." George Hadley put his hand up to shield off the burning light from his squinted eyes. "A zebra or a baby giraffe, maybe."

"Are you sure?" His wife sounded peculiarly tense.

"No, it's a little late to be sure," he said amused. "Nothing over there I can see but cleaned bone, and the vultures dropping for what's left."

"Did you hear that scream?" she asked.

"No."

"About a minute ago?"

"Sorry, no."

The lions were coming. And again George Hadley was filled with admiration for the mechanical genius who had conceived this room. A miracle of efficiency selling for an absurdly low price. Every home should have one. Oh, occasionally they frightened you with their clinical accuracy, they startled you, gave you a twinge, but most of the time what fun for everyone —not only for your own son and daughter, but for yourself when you felt like a quick jaunt to a foreign land, a quick change of scenery. Well, here it was!

And here were the lions now, fifteen feet away, so real, so feverishly and startlingly real that you could feel the prickling fur on your hand, and your mouth was stuffed with the dusty upholstery smell of their heated pelts, and the yellow of them was in your eyes likes the yellow of an exquisite French tapestry, the yellows of lions and summer grass, and the sound of the matted lion lungs exhaling on the silent noontide, and the smell of meat from the panting, dripping mouths.

The lions stood looking at George and Lydia Hadley with terrible green-yellow eyes.

"Watch out!" screamed Lydia.

The lions came running at them.

Lydia bolted and ran. Instinctively, George sprang after her. Outside, in the hall, with the door slammed, he was laughing and she was crying, and they both stood appalled at the other's reaction.

"George!"

"Lydia! Oh, my dear poor sweet Lydia!"

"They almost got us!"

"Walls, Lydia, remember; crystal walls, that's all they are. Oh, they look real, I must admit—Africa in your parlor—but it's all dimensional superreactionary, supersensitive color film and mental tape film behind glass screens. It's all odorophonics and sonics, Lydia. Here's my handkerchief."

"I'm afraid." She came to him and put her body against him and cried steadily. "Did you see? Did you *feel*? It's too real."

"Now Lydia . . ."

"You've got to tell Wendy and Peter not to read any more on Africa."

"Of course—of course." He patted her.

"Promise?"

"Sure."

"And lock the nursery for a few days until I get my nerves settled."

"You know how difficult Peter is about that. When I punished him a month ago by locking the nursery for even a few hours, the tantrum he threw! And Wendy too. They *live* for the nursery."

"It's got to be locked, that's all there is to it."

"All right." Reluctantly he locked the huge door. "You've been working too hard. You need a rest."

"I don't know—I don't know," she said, blowing her nose, sitting down in a chair that immediately began to rock and comfort her. "Maybe I don't have enough to do. Maybe I have time to think too much. Why don't we shut the whole house off for a few days and take a vacation?"

"You mean you want to fry my eggs for me?"

"Yes." She nodded.

"And darn my socks?"

"Yes." A frantic, watery-eyed nodding.

"And sweep the house?"

"Yes, yes—oh, yes!"

"But I thought that's why we bought this house, so we wouldn't have to do anything?"

"That's just it. I feel like I don't belong here. The house is wife and mother now, and nursemaid. Can I compete with an African veldt? Can I give a bath and scrub the children as efficiently or quickly as the automatic scrub bath can? I cannot. And it isn't just me. It's you. You've been awfully nervous lately."

"I suppose I have been smoking too much."

"You look as if you didn't know what to do with yourself in this house, either. You smoke a little more every morning and drink a little more every afternoon and need a little more sedative every night. You're beginning to feel unnecessary, too."

"Am I?" He paused and tried to feel into himself to see what was really there.

"Oh, George!" She looked beyond him, at the nursery door. "Those lions can't get out of there, can they?"

He looked at the door and saw it tremble as if something had jumped against it from the other side.

"Of course not," he said.

At dinner they ate alone, for Wendy and Peter were at a special plastic carnival across town and had televised home to say they'd be late, to go ahead eating. So George Hadley, bemused, sat watching the dining-room table produce warm dishes of food from its mechanical interior.

"We forgot the ketchup," he said.

"Sorry," said a small voice within the table, and ketchup appeared.

As for the nursery, thought George Hadley, it won't hurt for the children to be locked out of it a while. Too much of anything isn't good for anyone. And it was clearly indicated that the children had been spending a little to much time on Africa. That *sun*. He could feel it on his neck, still, like a hot paw. And the *lions*. And the smell of blood. Remarkable how the nursery caught the telepathic emanations of the children's minds and created life to fill their every desire. The children thought lions, and there were lions. The children thought zebras, and there were zebras. Sun—sun. Giraffes—giraffes. Death and death.

That *last*. He chewed tastelessly on the meat that the table had cut for him. Death thoughts. They were awfully young, Wendy and Peter, for death thoughts. Or, no, you were never too young, really. Long before you knew what death was you were wishing it on someone else. When you were two years old you were shooting people with cap pistols.

But this—the long, hot African veldt, the awful death in the jaws of a lion. And repeated again and again.

"Where are you going?"

He didn't answer Lydia. Preoccupied, he let the lights glow softly on ahead of him, extinguish behind him as he padded to the nursery door. He listened against it. Far away, a lion roared.

He unlocked the door and opened it. Just before he stepped inside, he heard a faraway scream. And then another roar from the lions, which subsided quickly.

He stepped into Africa. How many times in the last year had he opened this door and found Wonderland, Alice, the Mock Turtle, or Aladdin and his magical lamp, or Jack Pumpkinhead of Oz, or Dr. Doolittle, or the cow jumping over a very real-appearing moon—all the delightful contraptions of a make-believe world. How often had he seen Pegasus flying in the sky ceiling, or seen fountains of red fireworks, or heard angel voices singing. But now, this yellow hot Africa, this bake oven with murder in the heat . . . Perhaps Lydia was right. Perhaps they needed a little vacation from the fantasy which was growing a bit too real for ten-year-old children. It was all right to exercise one's mind with gymnastic fantasies, but when the lively child mind settled on *one* pattern . . . ? It seemed that at a distance for the past month he had heard lions roaring and smelled their strong odor seeping as far away as his study door. But, being busy, he had paid it no attention.

George Hadley stood on the African grassland alone. The lions looked up from their feeding, watching him. The only flaw to the illusion was the open door through which he could see his wife, far down the dark hall, like a framed picture, eating her dinner abstractedly.

"Go away," he said to the lions.

They did not go.

He knew the principle of the room exactly. You sent out your thoughts. Whatever you thought would appear.

"Let's have Aladdin and his lamp," he snapped.

The veldtland remained; the lions remained.

"Come on, room! I demand Aladdin!" he said.

Nothing happened. The lions mumbled in their baked pelts.

"Aladdin!"

He went back to dinner. "The fool room's out of order," he said. "It won't respond."

"Or . . ."

"Or what?"

"Or it *can't* respond," said Lydia, "because the children have thought about Africa and lions and killing so many days that the room's in a rut."

"Could be."

"Or Peter's set it to remain that way."

"*Set* it?"

"He may have got into the machinery and fixed something."

3

4

5

« *Quand la couleur est à sa richesse, la forme est à sa plénitude.* »

3 Cézanne, *Madame Cézanne dans la serre*, huile sur toile, 1890. New York, The Metropolitan Museum of Art.

4 Cézanne, *Portrait de Louis-Auguste Cézanne lisant* L'Événement, huile sur toile, 1866. Washington, National Gallery of Art.

5 Cézanne, portrait du fils de l'artiste, études pour *Mardi Gras*, crayon et lavis. Paris, musée du Louvre.

6 Cézanne, *Achille Emperaire*, huile sur toile, vers 1868. Paris, musée d'Orsay.

7 Cézanne, *Victor Choquet*, huile sur toile, 1876-1877. Collection particulière.

8 Cézanne, *Ambroise Vollard*, huile sur toile, 1899. Paris, musée du Petit Palais.